Play the Brazilian Way

The Secret Skills of the
World's Greatest Footballers

Play the Brazilian Way

The Secret Skills of the
World's Greatest Footballers

Simon Clifford

BOXTREE

First published in 1999 by Boxtree, an imprint of Macmillan Publishers Ltd,
25 Eccleston Place, London, SW1W 9NF and Basingstoke

Associated companies throughout the world

ISBN 0 7522 21347 4

3 5 7 9 8 6 4 2

A CIP catalogue record for this book is available from the British Library

Photographs © Anton Want 1998, except pages 13 © Mitre, pages 11, 14,
17, 18, 58, 60, 61, 66 (bottom), 67, 70, 71, 76 & 80 courtesy of
Coloursport, 24 & 78 courtesy of Allsport,
and pages 8, 20, 90 & 92 author's own

Typeset by Neal Townsend

Printed in Great Britain by the Bath Press, Bath

Contents

Prologue

AFTER MANY YEARS of lofty isolation, England joined FIFA and competed in the World Cup in 1950. The tournament was held in Brazil and England's results were poor, most notoriously in Belo Horizonte where they were humiliated by a 1–0 defeat at the hands of the USA. Although Uruguay won the competition it was the Brazilians, the runners-up, who were considered by most who watched the tournament to be the best footballing team. On their return from Brazil the English FA produced a report suggesting that much could be learned from the Brazilian training methods:

> To all from the United Kingdom who watched the tournament it was clearly evident that many of the competing countries, especially those from South America about whom we knew the least, had made tremendous progress. The Brazilian team's football was accurate, skilful and fast. Their game is attractive to watch, differing in many respects from that seen in this country. On three successive occasions I saw them play football of bewildering skill against opposition I had previously ranked as good. I cannot remember having seen a better side.
>
> Watching young Brazilians at their training grounds, they had a fairly long period of practice before they started games under the watchful eye of the coach. We were informed that they were beginners yet their control and skill was phenomenal for their age. This enthusiasm for training, practice and disciplined coaching is typical of football throughout Brazil.
>
> There is no copyright to fitness and skill, but the resources and energy of the South American countries have set them in a strong position to challenge Britain and Europe in competitive play.

The FA report recommended that a committee be formed with the purpose of examining Brazilian training methods. The 'Technical Committee' was formed, but met only once and decided that it was not necessary to take any further action.

Eight years later, after Brazil had taken the 1958 World Cup, the legendary English player Tom Finney remarked:

Can we in Britain profit from the Brazilian lesson? Of course. Do we wish to learn from Brazil? I doubt it, although I feel that it is essential that we should. The very idea of learning from foreigners will seem unpalatable to many of the old school, but the days have long gone where England was the masters of football and the rest of the world pupils. We are too conservative in our ideas in this country. Anything new is regarded with suspicion, while the old methods, although out of date, are always trusted. Where we fall down in our training – and this applies to both club and country – is in our work with the ball. Training must be scientifically planned. It must be organized and supervised from start to finish as it is in Brazil. Skill can be brought out and improved, provided the correct methods are followed.

Television viewers marvelled when they saw the fabulous Didi taking a free kick with the outside of his foot. He did not accidentally master the art of making the ball swerve. He worked and worked through practice until it was perfect. What became of the panel of experts [The FA committee set up in 1950]? They met once and were never heard of again. So a wonderful idea remained just an idea.

Finney was ahead of his time. In the forty years that have passed since he made these remarks, Brazilian footballers have continued to stun the world with their skills, yet the British football community has made little effort to discover or emulate their training techniques. The Premier League clubs seem content to buy the skilled players from abroad rather than create them and the British game still lacks the technique and skill seen in other countries.

In 1997 Simon Clifford went to Brazil to find out what the FA should have uncovered all those years ago in 1950 – what makes the Brazilians such brilliant footballers. Now he has brought this information back to England and started to train young players in techniques Brazilian football clubs and schools use. The results could revolutionize British football, and finally bring the beautiful game back to its birthplace.

Introduction

Children at the Ayrton Senna Soccer School in São Paulo playing futebol de salão

FOOTBALL SUPPORTERS all over the world marvel at the way Brazilian footballers play. The breathtaking skill, explosive shooting, precision passing and incredible ball control make Brazilian footballers unquestionably the world's best. World Cup champions on no less than four occasions and runners-up twice, the Brazilians continually produce players that the rest of the world can only stand and admire.

What makes Brazilians such good footballers? The romantic view held by many outsiders is that the players are naturals who developed their skills on the streets of São Paulo and the beaches of Rio de Janeiro. It's true that football is played everywhere in Brazil, where the game is a nationwide passion. But the real key to the country's success lies in the way the players are trained and the specific skills they are taught under the supervision of coaches and teachers in schools and clubs.

In 1992 I wrote to the FA asking for advice on Brazilian training methods and enquiring if any books were available on them in this country. The FA replied that they had no information to give on the subject.

In 1995 Juninho's transfer to Middlesbrough brought a taste of the Brazilian style to the Premier League. His time at Middlesbrough was marked by his magical control and skill on the ball and his ability to bring it under control with any part of his body with just one touch, no matter which direction the ball was coming from or which way he was facing. His ability to send opponents the wrong way and to skip over challenges in the tightest of spaces was something we had never seen before from a player in this country.

As a Middlesbrough fan, and a football coach trying to find out about Brazilian training methods, I was fortunate enough to have the chance to meet Juninho and talk to him about how he learned to play such beautiful football.

Juninho always attributed his skills to his training in Brazil, and particularly the playing of a game called *futebol de salão*. Juninho told me that almost all of the great Brazilian players of the past, including Pelé, Rivelino and Romário, had been brought up playing this game.

I was fascinated by Juninho's skills, and by what he told me about how they were learned. So I decided to set

'If you train in the way described in this book, you will learn to play as I did, and as Pelé did and Garrincha before him. You will learn to play as a Brazilian plays with skill, style, finesse and beauty. It's the only way to play'

Juninho

out on a journey of discovery, to find out for myself just what Juninho was talking about and to bring back whatever I could in an effort to enhance the English game with Brazilian skills. So it was that, with borrowed money and not a little trepidation, I flew to Brazil. I travelled with the BBC who made a TV documentary about my trip called *A Whole New Ball Game*.

In Brazil I met some of the greatest players of the world who are now passing their own knowledge on to a new generation of youngsters. I talked to Zico, Careca, Rivelino and, the most famous of them all, Pelé. Each one of them confirmed what Juninho had told me about Brazilian training techniques and *futebol de salão*.

I spent time with São Paulo FC, whose approach to their young players surprised me, having been told for so long by all the experts that the Brazilians are born footballers and that they are just naturally gifted. Nothing could be further from the truth. The reality is that Brazilian clubs spend a great deal of time and energy working with young players. Their youngsters live at the club, going to school either in the morning or afternoon and spending the other half of the day learning football. Their weight is monitored, their diets are individually assessed week by week, they have all manner of support staff – physiotherapists, warm-up coaches, warm-down coaches, doctors, dietitians, trainers, tactical coaches – all dedicated to producing the talented players of the future. They work for hours on exercises to develop the tricks and skills that seem so natural and spontaneous on the pitch. Luck doesn't come into it. It's science, hard work and dedication. And not least, a game called *futebol de salão*.

Futebol de salão is unique to Brazil. It's a five-a-side game played on an area the size of a basketball court. The size two ball used for the game is smaller than a conventional football and filled with foam, which means

Juninho playing for Brazil against England in the 1995 Umbro Cup

> *'Everything I had as a*
>
> *Brazilian player I owed*
>
> *to* futebol de salão'
>
> **Zico**

it is heavier and doesn't bounce above the ankle. The weight, size and lack of bounce of the ball, and the small size of the court, demand greater concentration and accuracy from the players and place the emphasis on the developing of skilful dribbling, precision passing and ball control – skills for which Brazilian players are so well known.

All of the legendary Brazilian players and even modern greats like Ronaldo, Denílson and Juninho played *futebol de salão* as children. For most Brazilian national team players, it is the only game they played in their formative years. They all agree that this is the most important factor that distinguishes Brazilian players from those in the rest of the world.

I was so impressed by what I had seen and heard in Brazil that on my return, I decided to set up an organization in England to bring *futebol de salão* and Brazilian training methods to a new and, it turned out, enthusiastic and receptive audience. Feedback from people I knew in the game was extremely positive and I had no difficulty in attracting youngsters to come to training sessions using the methods and routines I had learned. The training uses *futebol de salão* and conventional balls and focuses on precision passing, playing the ball on the floor, avoiding long, speculative passes for the big lads to chase and general emphasis on ways to attack and break down the opposition. The results were staggering and in a short while a team of local boys trained with my methods were able to hold their own against a team of youth players training at a Premiership club. Several of my young players have already received approaches from Premiership clubs.

Interest was such that I decided to leave my teaching job to set up a national organization, the UK Confederation of Futebol de Salão, and its sister organization, Brazilian Soccer Schools.

The response from the football community has been tremendous, with almost all the Premier League clubs expressing a desire to find out more. At the time of publication, Premier League club Middlesbrough has already established *futebol de salão* as an integral part of its training regime. Their coaches attended a day session with me at my Brazilian Soccer School and a regular contact arrangement has been instigated. It will be the first of many such arrangements.

There was interest too from sports manufacturers and I struck a deal with Mitre to produce the *futebol de salão* ball. This deal has made my dream a reality as *futebol de salão* balls are now available in all good sports stores.

The BBC have continued to follow my progress and joined me when I returned to Brazil in 1998, when I took a team of my players to train and play with the Brazilian stars of the future in São Paulo soccer schools. This year, a group of Brazilian street children will be coming to England to train and play with us. Perhaps we will even be able to teach them something new!

Football was taken to Brazil by an Englishman. The Brazilians are about to return the compliment.

The **futebol de salão** *ball is considerably smaller than a conventional football*

Class of '58, the first Brazilian team to lift the World Cup

THE FOUNDER OF FOOTBALL in Brazil was a man called Charles Miller, who was born in São Paulo in 1874 to English parents. As a young boy he was sent to England to go to school. At the time football was just becoming popular in England and it was played at Miller's school in Southampton. Miller excelled at the game and when he left school he began playing in the Southampton amateur leagues. He was a very good player, renowned for his dribbling.

EVENTUALLY MILLER returned to São Paulo to work on the railways but he was determined to continue playing the game that he loved. He knew from correspondence with his family that football was not played in Brazil. So before returning to São Paulo, he packed his case with an FA rulebook, two footballs and two sets of football kit. These were the tools with which Miller founded the game in Brazil.

Miller had a missionary zeal to see the game of football prosper in Brazil. It was first played at the São Paulo Athletic Club in 1894. Organized leagues soon followed in the late 1890s in São Paulo – where for the first three years Miller was the leading scorer – and Rio de Janeiro. The founding clubs in São Paulo were São Paulo Athletic Club, Mackenzie, Internacional, Germania, Corinthians Paulista, Juventus, Palestra Italia, Ipiranga, Clube Atletico Paulistano and finally the São Paulo Railway (SPR). In Rio de Janeiro Fluminense, Flamengo, América, Bangu, Vasco da Gama, Rio Grande do Sul and Grêmio were the founding teams. In these two cities, football prospered and later spread to other areas of Brazil.

Before long, Brazil was taking its own special brand of football to the international stage. Brazil played its first international game in 1914 and in 1938 they reached the semi-finals of the World Cup, losing to Italy. The São Paulo striker Leônidas da Silva was the top scorer of the tournament.

The next World Cup, in 1950, was held in Brazil. The whole country was transfixed by the tournament, and expectations were high. This time the national team reached the final, losing 2–1 to Uruguay. The English FA, having entered a team in the World Cup for the first time, saw in the Brazilian team an exciting new style that should have been emulated.

In 1958 the Brazilian national team boasted players who were to become legends: Didi, Vavá, Garrincha, and the seventeen-year-old Pelé, who was perhaps the finest footballer the world has ever seen. That year Brazil lifted the Jules Rimet trophy, proving that they had truly arrived as a world footballing power.

Brazil went on to retain the trophy in 1962 in Chile and again in 1970 in Mexico. The peerless 1970 team, which included Pelé, Rivelino, Tostão, Gerson, Jairzinho and Carlos Alberto, is remembered by the thousands who saw them in Mexico and the millions who watched in wonder on televisions around the world as the greatest team of all time.

The 1970 team summed up what Pelé described so aptly as 'the beautiful game'. Each player had breathtaking ball skills and creativity and with their one-touch passes, little flicks, and explosive dribbles they seemed to create the time and space in which to work their magic. Theirs was the ultimate attacking game and the attack could come from anywhere, even from their defenders, marshalled by Carlos Alberto. The team were not tied to rigid formations and seemed to break all the rules, yet they worked together so smoothly that it seemed as if they were reading each other's minds. In fact, this was not instinctive play, the players had spent months preparing for the World Cup. The team that took to the field in Guadalajara was perhaps the best prepared in the history of football. Commentator John Motson remarked, 'They were all of our football dreams come true.' After winning the trophy three times, Brazil retained the Jules Rimet trophy in perpetuity.

Over the next ten years Brazil remained a force in national football, reaching the semi-finals of the 1974 and 1978 World Cups. For the 1982 World Cup, Brazil again produced an outstanding team which enchanted the watching world. However, the team, which included Zico, Socrates, Junior, Eder and Falcão, was cruelly beaten 3–2 by the eventual winners, Italy, in the quarter-final. A team which many in Brazil considered to be one of the all-time greats had failed to win the ultimate prize.

In 1994 in the USA a more tactically aware team balanced the natural exuberance of the Brazilian game with the realities of modern international football. But Romário and Bebeto maintained the great Brazilian tradition of players who had the ability to light up the world's foremost tournament with sublime attacking skills as Brazil became the first and only team to win the World Cup four times.

In 1998 Brazil sought to retain their title in France. After progressing steadily, if not exactly sensationally, through all the qualifying games, everyone expected the Brazilians to take their fifth title against a French side which appeared to be struggling to score goals. Brazil's coach, Zagallo, appeared to have confounded the criticism from home for relying on the old warhorses Dunga, Bebeto and Leonardo, stars of the 1994 victory, at the expense of the world's most expensive footballer, Denílson, and other promising newcomers. It was Zagallo's proud boast that he had been involved in all of Brazil's World Cup triumphs, as a player in 1958 and 1962, and as coach in 1970 and 1994. His day of reckoning was to come in the 1998 final with the mysterious affair surrounding the FIFA World Footballer of the Year – Ronaldo.

What exactly happened in the hotel prior to the final is still shrouded in half-truths, but it would appear that Ronaldo had some kind of a fit and perhaps shouldn't have played. Play he did, however, and the performance of the Brazilian team was well below the standards even of this much criticized selection. The players were out of sorts, and in the end were well beaten by the home team. Zagallo paid the price when he was dismissed after the tournament, much to the delight of a large section of the Brazilian population who had accused him of sacrificing 'the beautiful game' in pursuit of a method which had his supremely talented individuals functioning as badly oiled cogs in a machine.

The defeat in France devastated the

The peerless 1970 team, true exponents of the beautiful game

Brazilian nation. For Brazilians football is not just a sport, it is an art form and almost a religion. The national team are often described as the heartbeat of the nation. When the team plays people feel that the national identity of Brazil is being displayed on the field.

There is no doubt that Brazil continues to produce outstanding players. Brazilian footballers are the most sought after in the world. Denílson's £26 million transfer from São Paulo to Real Betis eclipsed the previous world record of Ronaldo's £18 million transfer to Inter Milan. The question after the defeat in France was whether

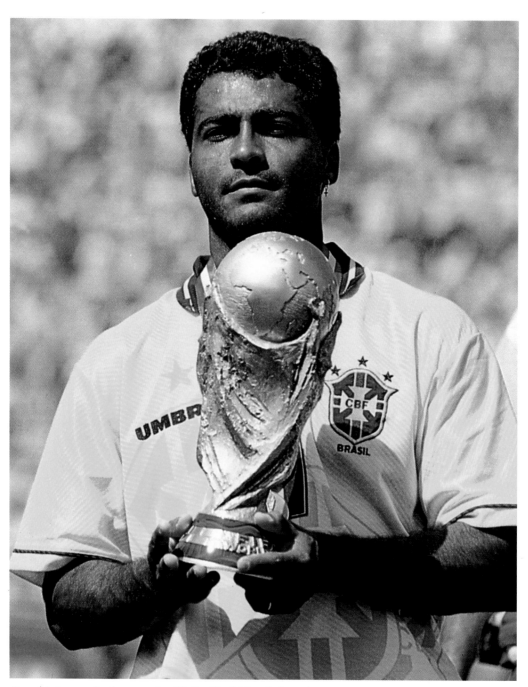

Romário's proudest moment, with the World Cup in America, 1994

Brazilian football needed to change. Should Brazil imitate European national teams with their more defensive play, or revert to the style of its past.

It was a question that did not need answering. To imitate the Europeans would be to sacrifice the spectacle of beautiful football, which to Brazilians has always been as important as winning. The famous yellow shirt represents passion, grace and guile, and that is why they remain everyone's favourites. (Brazil are many people's second-favourite national team after their own country. In England, Brazilian shirts actually outsold England shirts during France 98.)

Brazil is looking back to learn lessons from its own glorious past in order to rediscover the joy of playing the game without constraints or rigid tactics. The desire in Brazil from the people and the new national coach is to return to a purer age, where commercialism and sponsorship could not dim the magnificent radiance of *o amerelo camisa*, the yellow jersey.

A sense of hope has replaced the disappointment of France 98. The Brazilian people are looking ahead to the 2002 World Cup when they believe that the *penta*, the fifth triumph, will be realized. Looking at the young players continuing to emerge in Brazil, few would doubt that the dream of the *penta* will become a reality.

The 1970 team summed up what Pelé described so aptly as 'the beautiful game' ... The team that took to the field in Guadalajara was perhaps the best prepared in the history of football. Commentator John Motson remarked, 'They were all of our football dreams come true'

The author playing beach football in Rio

MANY MYTHS ABOUND about what produces what is seen as the 'samba star' – the Brazilian player with extravagant flair. For many years, the common perception of the typical Brazilian footballer was that he graduated from playing on the beach or in the streets with rag balls or oranges straight into the national team and World Cup glory. It is often said that the great poverty in Brazil compels the young to practise football as an escape route from the *favelas*, the poorest areas of the city; that they are naturally gifted; that they have nothing else to do; that it's the samba rhythm we can never hope to capture; that it's in their genes. True analysis shows that while these theories may possibly go a small way towards explaining Brazil's continued success, they are by no means the full answer. So how do Brazilians learn their unique style of football?

THE STREET

Pelé, like many of the Brazilian greats, first played football in the backstreets of his home town, Tres Coracões in Minas Gerais, using a small orange as a substitute for a football, which only the wealthy could afford. Others, such as Rivelino, would use a stuffed sock. However, very soon these players graduated to training centres with the major clubs. The street may have been where they got their first taste of football, but it was certainly not where their skills were honed. For the past twenty years, talented Brazilian children have barely played in the streets at all. They are trained for up to twenty hours per week by the professional football clubs or soccer schools.

When I asked 1970 World Cup champion Rivelino about the myth of learning the game on the streets he said: 'Kids don't play in the streets any more. In the cities, they build everywhere. There is no room for them to kick a ball. The kids learn on the smaller *futebol de salão* courts. Small-sided games are better for developing skills. Because there is no space, players have to learn to think faster. You have to learn to control the ball instantly, and to pass it quickly. This is where the street players of today show their art.'

THE BEACH

In Rio de Janeiro and the Santos area of São Paulo, people enjoy the pleasures of beach life throughout the year. Volleyball, water-skiing, swimming, sailing, windsurfing and surfing are all popular. However, the most popular sports on the beach are *futevolei* and beach soccer.

Futevolei is played between two teams of five or six players divided by a net the height of a volleyball net. The players must keep the ball in the air using their feet and bodies, but not their hands or arms, to pass it between team members and over the net. The aim is to knock the ball over the net and on to the sand in the opposing team's playing area. A point is gained every time the ball hits the opponents' ground.

This game is great for developing first touch and the use of a variety of body areas to control the ball. The casual bystander in Rio watching a game is treated to a feast of football with the most unbelievable tricks and flicks that this game encourages on show. The game is not really popular with the younger players, but older players, even professionals, will often come down to the beach to play a game with friends as the sun is going down.

Beach football is a beach version of our own five-a-side football using a regular ball and goals. This game allows players to get a real feel of the ball, as it is played barefoot. The undulations of the sand teach players to cope and play with skill, even in the most difficult circumstances. In Brazil, beach football is played for fun and also in organized leagues. Former professional players make up a substantial proportion of the players in the higher standard leagues. Romário, star of the 1994 World Cup, is one of the greatest exponents and fans of beach football. Indeed, his absence from the Brazilian team in France 98 was caused by an injury sustained while playing beach football.

A more simple game played on the beach is juggling. A group of people will share a football, working together to keep the ball in the air, passing from one to the other without letting it touch the ground. The aim is to produce a more extravagant flick or technique than the player before. Again this is a wonderful way to develop first-touch skills.

However, while these beach games are popular in Brazil, few Brazilians would suggest that they have a major part to play in Brazil's continued football success. The beach games are more of a fun environment for the people to express their universal love of 'the beautiful game' or *jogo bonito*.

SAMBA

Music and dance are two potent ingredients of Brazilian life, and their influence is evident in their football. The rhythm of the great Brazilian teams has often been seen as a product of samba music, indigenous to Brazil. Samba has its roots in the rich African legacy of the early settlers in Rio de Janeiro. Many clubs and soccer schools teach ball skills to a background beat of samba. *Jinga* is the term Brazilians use to describe a dancer who moves with great fluidity, flexibility and smoothness. *Jinga* is evident in all of the great Brazilian players.

CAPOEIRA

Capoeira is a cross between a dance and a martial art practised in Brazil. It involves dancing using highly complex fighting movements to a background beat slower than the samba. Perhaps some of the movement and flexibility illustrated by Brazilian players has its roots in this type of dance.

SCHOOLS IN BRAZIL

Children go to school in Brazil between the ages of five and eighteen. *Futebol de salão* is a compulsory part of the curriculum and every school has its own court. In Brazil, no competition exists between schools in football, there are no leagues, championships or inter-school games. This means that the schools concentrate on developing ball skills rather than the tactics needed to win the next game.

BRAZILIAN CLUB FOOTBALL

The Brazilian football season lasts for most of the year, with only a small break in January. The system is based on four state leagues, which are contested between the end of January and May. The two most important state leagues are the Paulista, based around teams from São Paulo, and the Carioca, for the teams from Rio de Janeiro. When these league seasons are over, the qualifying teams play in a national league, the Brasileiro. The main reason for this system is the sheer size of Brazil – it is bigger in area than main continental USA, and although most of the population is concentrated along the Atlantic coast, the distances to travel are huge.

The Brazilian clubs have a wonderful structure for developing young players. The focus is on producing great players with wonderful skills, rather than buying them at inflated prices from other countries. Professional teams invest a much higher proportion of their revenue in youth development programmes than English clubs. The staff and content of these programmes are vastly superior to anything seen in other countries. The clubs have every conceivable facility – swimming pools, tennis courts, gymnasiums, clubhouses, restaurants, snack bars – and the children are well catered for. Many of the children board in the clubs as they may have come from families many hundreds, or even thousands of miles from the club.

Clubs take players from the age of six. For the first few years they will work only on ball skills, using the exercises explained later in this book, and *futebol de salão* games. Only when these skills are developed do they move on to tactics and eleven-a-side football. Ronaldo played *futebol de salão* until he was seventeen.

By the age of twelve, players will be training twenty hours a week – more than many professionals in England. This comprises five four-hour sessions per week.

SOCCER SCHOOLS

Many soccer schools run similar training programmes to the clubs – with regard to the time and quality of training – for the children who are not yet ready to train with the clubs. Former greats such as Rivelino, Careca and Zico all run soccer schools of their own and devote their time to producing the players of tomorrow.

We have looked at some of the many possible explanations for the success of Brazil in producing great footballers, but it seems that only two carry any true weight as meaningful ingredients that could be exported from Brazil to improve footballing skills around the world. *Futebol de salão* appears to be the most important, and all of the great players agree with this. But the other important factor is the club and soccer-school training. The drills and practices that the young players undertake, day in, day out, are quite distinct from anything seen in any other country. It is these practices that we will be looking at in the next section of the book. A combination of regular practice using these drills together with frequent *futebol de salão* games will result in a marked improvement of the skills of beginners and experienced players alike.

The head
Used to cushion the ball, pass or shoot (a header).

The chest
Used to pass or cushion the ball.

The thigh
Used to pass, cushion or shoot.

The knee
Used to pass, cushion or shoot.

How the different parts of the body are used to control the ball

FIRST TOUCH DESCRIBES the ability of a player to bring the ball under control with only one touch of the ball. It is something that Brazilian football is famous for and the exercises in this book will help you develop the skill. A good first touch will always leave the ball exactly where the player intends in order to execute the next move. The skilful player can use the head, chest, thigh or knee as well as all parts of the foot to control the ball with the first touch.

THE FOOT
The inside
This area is most often used for kicking, short dribbling and placing shots with greater accuracy.

The sole
Used in many moves to beat players and to control or pass the ball.

The instep
This part of the foot is used often for passing, chipping, shooting and curling.

The heel
Can be used to pass the ball over short distances.

The top
This is the most powerful area of the foot and is used for driving the ball long distances, shooting or clearing.

The outside
This area is used for bending and curling the ball. In Brazil it is known as the *trivella* and is used for short and long passes as well as shooting.

As well as understanding how different parts of the body can be used to control the ball, it's important to know the varying effects that can be achieved by kicking different areas of the ball:

THE BALL
The top
When the ball is struck hard from the top through to the bottom it will give the shot a dip effect. When the power from the strike decreases the ball spins forward, falling rapidly to the ground. This is an excellent way to beat a wall at free kicks as the ball should clear the wall then dip towards the goal.

The bottom
Used for chipping and striking the ball high over a long distance.

The sides
When you hit the side of the ball only it will swerve or bend to the left or right.

The middle
The middle of the ball is struck for medium-length mid-height passes and shots. The ball will stay low and can be hit with great power in this area.

There is no end to the variations to these basic rules. For example, kicking through the ball from top to bottom with the instep slightly to the left will produce a ball that will bend to the right, but sit up when it lands with a 'backspin' effect. These and other variations are looked at later in the book.

Remember that your body posture and the part of the foot and strength that you strike the ball with will also determine the effect that you have on the ball.

'Before the age of fifteen years the young player should not be at all concerned with tactics, defending or positional elements. The focus should be only on learning basic techniques. It should be ball, ball and more ball'

Zico

The rest of the book looks at how, through practice, you can learn to play with the same grace, finesse, skill and beauty as a Brazilian player. Remember that their skills are not natural, they are learned and honed through many, many hours of practice. Now, you can do the same.

By carefully following the instructions you will find that you quickly improve. Your individual skill will develop, as will your team play. Most of the exercises are for you to practise each day on your own. With regular practice you will develop the confidence to put these skills into your play in game situations. You must try to read the instructions for the exercise or skill you are attempting each time you practise.

These exercises focus on all of the basic techniques necessary for you to become a highly skilled attacking player. Tactics and defending are not looked at here although these are very important areas and, while Brazilians are not famed as great defenders or tacticians, their teams still practise for many hours on these vital parts of the game. However, the focus for the young player should be to develop his or her skills, working on beating opponents, shooting, passing, heading and dribbling. These are the elements of the game that have made Brazil the country of 'the beautiful game'. With practice you too can play beautiful football.

THE WARM-UP SHOULD last fifteen to twenty minutes. In Brazil it is usually done to music, often samba. This helps the players to get into a rhythm for the game. The warm-up is very similar to a dance and allows the players to develop great flexibility in the hips and around the knees, which is vital if you are to move and play as the Brazilians do. These exercises are best done over an area of around fifty metres: running the length of a gym or across a football pitch is ideal.

1 Jog for fifty metres at a very slow pace.

2 Turn back and skip, with your body turned to the side.

3 Skip again facing forward and swinging your arms alternately above your head.

4 Skip again, this time swinging the arms alternately across your body.

5 Jog for four strides then touch the floor with the left hand, jog four more strides and touch the floor with the right hand. Repeat every four strides.

6 Jog for four strides, then leap high as though you are heading an imaginary football. Repeat after every four strides.

7 Jog for two strides and move to strike an imaginary ball with your right foot. After another two strides kick with your left foot. Repeat every two strides.

8 Run backward, pushing your feet back and up through the air in an exaggerated style.

9 Jog two small steps then kick your right leg as high as you can, clapping your hands as you kick. Repeat with your left leg after two more steps. This exercise should be done to a rhythm. If you are doing this with your team-mates it may help for one person to count out loud to help the others keep time.

10 Repeat exercise 9, but instead of high kicks lift the knee to hip height then swing it out to the side, alternating legs every two strides.

It is vital to warm up properly before training sessions and games. Warming up loosens the muscles, helping to avoid injury through tears and strains

Hamstring stretch: stretch slowly, reaching down towards the toes

THE NEXT PART OF any training session should be stretching. As well as helping to prevent injuries to your muscles stretching gives you a greater range of movement and will improve and extend what you are able to do with the ball.

Before you start any stretching it is important that you have first warmed up. This raises your body temperature and your heart rate, warming the muscles. You should never stretch a muscle when it is cold.

Hamstrings

The hamstrings are the group of muscles at the back of your thigh. Sit on the floor with your legs stretched out in front of you. Stretching your arms along your legs, bend slowly over, moving your hands down your legs as you bend.

When you reach your ankles hold for ten seconds, then slowly sit back up. Repeat five times.

Quadriceps

The quadriceps are the muscles at the front of the thigh. Standing straight, grab one foot and lift it up behind you, bending the knee, so that your foot touches your backside. Hold this position for ten seconds and repeat five times, then change legs. If it is difficult to balance put your free hand on the shoulder of another player.

Calf

Press your palms against a wall or the palms of another player. Stretch one leg out behind you, and bend the knee of the other leg. Keep both feet pointing forward and your soles flat on the ground.

Groin

This exercise works the calf and groin muscles. Stand up straight, then stretch the left leg back behind you, balancing on the ball of your left foot. Bend both knees but don't allow the left knee to touch the ground. Put your hands on your hips and hold steady for ten seconds. Do five of these and then repeat with the right leg.

Legs are the footballer's most useful tools. However, when you are warming up you must not forget the upper half of the body.

Stomach

Lie on the ground with your hands by your shoulders in the press-up position. Push up slowly, lifting the body. Hold for ten seconds, then lower the body. Repeat six times.

Side

Stand with your legs apart, place your right arm above your head and the left arm behind your back. Bend to the left, stretching from your right arm through the right side of the body. Don't bend forward or back. Your move should be slow and gentle. Hold the stretch for ten seconds and repeat four times. Then repeat on the other side.

Hips

The hips give your body a wide range of movement and need to be flexible. Stand up straight, with your legs relaxed and your hands on your hips. Push the hips out to the left, then to the front, then to the right and the back, completing a full circle. The aim is to achieve a smooth, rolling motion. Repeat five times, then switch direction, rolling the hips from right to left.

> **IT IS IMPORTANT TO REMEMBER THE FOLLOWING:**
> - **Don't rush into any of the stretches**
> - **Avoid sharp, quick movements, make sure the stretches are smooth**
> - **Don't overstretch, hold the position for ten seconds and then repeat**
> - **Don't hold your breath during the stretch, breathe normally**
> - **Stop straight away if you feel any sharp pain**

Quadriceps stretch

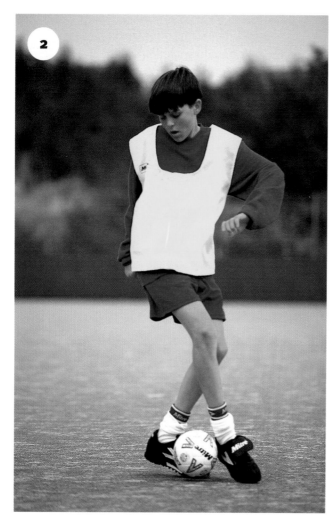

The player swings the right leg in front of the ball anti-clockwise, then the left leg clockwise in a fast and fluid movement

AFTER THE INITIAL warm-up and stretches, the next step is to begin working with the ball. Warming up with the ball allows you to improve your touch, control and feel of the ball.

Spend about two minutes on each of these exercises. At first walk through the movements step by step then gradually pick up speed, trying to make each movement as fluid as possible.

1 Place the ball in front of you and swing your left leg around the front of the ball, moving clockwise. Then do the same with the right foot moving anticlockwise. Repeat, speeding up the movements and developing a rhythm, so that you are making a figure of eight with your feet. Try to bend the knees and move the hips in order to stay low over the ball for better balance. As you practise you will find this becomes easier and smoother. Remember to lift your head and not to look down at the ball. Soon you will be dancing around the ball.

2 Place the ball in front of you. Swing the left leg around the ball anticlockwise and across the right leg. Swing the right leg forward and around the ball clockwise, crossing over the left leg. Repeat.

3 Place the ball in front of you and with a jogging movement touch the top of the ball with the sole of each foot alternately. The ball should not move. Keep your head up and pump your arms as though you are sprinting.

4 Jog on the ball as above, but turn your foot so that it points outward each time it touches the ball. This develops flexibility in your feet and ankles.

5 Next, the reverse: land on the ball with the sole of the foot but toes pointing inward.

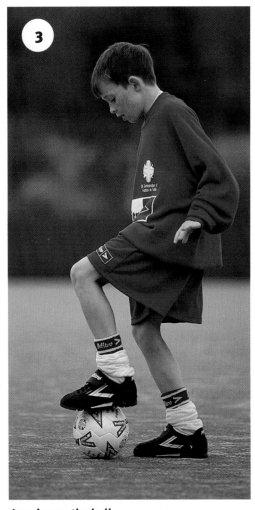

Jogging on the ball

6 With the ball in front of you use the sole of the right foot to drag it towards you. As the ball rolls towards you, tap it gently forward with the inside of your right foot. Catch the ball as it is going away from your body with your left foot and drag it back towards the body with the sole of your left foot. As the ball reaches you tap out gently with the inside of your left foot and catch it again with the right foot, repeating the movement from the start. Try developing this drill so that you do the drag back and tap forward in one smooth movement.

7 Using the middle of the sole of the right foot drag the ball from right to left, across your body. Catch the ball with the left foot and, using the middle of the sole, drag the ball from left to right and repeat.

8 With one foot roll the ball from side to side in front of you, using both sides of the sole to control the ball. Your foot should not leave the ball at any point. Repeat with the other foot.

Exercise 6: the player drags the ball towards him with the sole before tapping it out with the inside of the foot

9 Place the ball in front of you. With the right foot, step across the ball and the left leg, so that your legs are crossed (a). Swing the left leg around in front of the right, pivoting on the right leg (b), and tap the ball. After one minute change the kicking foot.

10 Using the side of the foot push the ball forward as if you were passing it (a), extending your leg as far as it will go in front of you. Before releasing the ball catch it with the sole of the same foot (b). Drag the ball back on to the other foot and repeat. With practice this can be repeated quickly and is an excellent move to deceive an opponent in a game.

11 Tap the ball to the side with the inside of the right foot and back with the inside of the left. Remember to keep your head up, increase the speed and see how many touches you are able to make in one minute.

12 Drag the ball back towards the body with the sole of the foot, then tap the ball forward with the sole of the same foot. Stop the ball with the inside of the same foot and jump over the ball, turning as you do, so that you are facing the ball in the opposite direction when you land. Repeat this exercise with the other foot. An alternative exercise is to flick the ball behind you as you jump and turn rather than stopping it.

13 Drag the ball across the body with the sole of one foot then tap it back with the side of the opposite foot, repeat for one minute, and then change feet.

14 Tap the ball with the inside of the right foot, then with the outside of the left, then the inside of the left and, finally, the outside of the right. Then repeat.

15 Place the ball in front of you. Using the right foot drag the ball towards your body. With the inside of your right foot tap the ball behind your left leg. Catch the ball with the sole of your left foot and drag it back across the body to the starting position. Then repeat.

16 Tap the ball to the side with the inside of one foot (a) and then back with the outside of the same foot (b), remaining on the spot and repeat. The standing leg's foot should pivot as you touch the ball.

All of these moves can be executed with greater and greater speed as you get more confident. Set yourself tests – for example, try to perform 100 repetitions of a particular movement without a mistake. Movements 2 to 16 can be performed moving the ball and yourself around the area in which you are working.

The keys to these exercises are fast feet, getting in as many touches of the ball as you can and remembering to keep your head up. This is good practice for game situations when you will need to keep your eyes on your team-mates in order to evaluate your passing options. You will notice that when you look straight ahead with the ball at your feet you can still see the ball out of the bottom of your eyes.

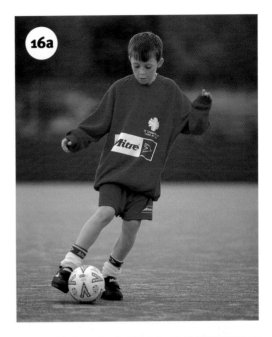

Exercise 16: good movement from the hips is essential in this exercise

Keep your eyes on the ball and use your arms for balance

IN A GAME the ball will come at you from a variety of heights, from differing distances and at a range of speeds. For these reasons it is vital that as well as being skilled at controlling the ball on the ground, you are also able to bring the ball under control when it comes to you through the air. You need to develop the ability to make first-touch passes in these situations or to bring the ball immediately to the ground in order to pass, shoot or dribble with the ball. The following exercises help to develop these skills. For each of these exercises you need to work with a partner, standing five metres apart and taking it in turns to supply the ball, changing after five or ten repetitions.

Breathing in when receiving the ball on the chest will help you control the ball

1 Player one throws the ball to player two at head height. Player two heads the ball back for player one to catch. As you gain greater control, you can try simply to head the ball back and forth between each other. Remember when heading to keep your eyes open, your arms wide for balance, and to throw the top of your body forward to produce power. You should hit the ball with your forehead.

2 Player one throws the ball to player two at chest height. Player two cushions the ball with his chest, and, as it falls, volleys the ball with the inside of the foot back to the thrower. The ball should not be allowed to bounce on the ground.

3 Again, player one throws the ball to player two's chest. This time player two throws his chest out, pushing the ball back to his partner with a chest pass.

4 Player one throws the ball to player two's knee. Player two catches the ball on his knee, flicks it on to the inside of the foot of the same leg and volleys the ball back to the thrower.

5 Again player one throws the ball to player two's knee (a). This time player two catches the ball with one knee and flicks it to the other knee, then volleys the ball back with the knee (b).

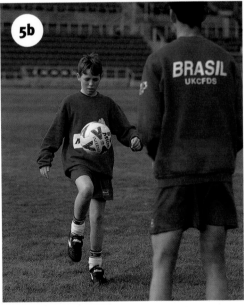

Relax the body as the ball approaches. A tense player will not control the ball well

6 Player one passes to player two's feet. Player two catches the ball with the instep of one foot, flicks it to the instep of the other foot and returns the ball.

7 Again the ball is passed to the feet. This time player two catches it on the top of the foot, on the laces, flicks the ball to the top of the other foot, and returns it.

8 This time the ball is volleyed straight back to the thrower, using the inside of the foot.

9 The ball is returned using the outside of the foot.

10 This time, player two faces away from player one, still standing five metres apart. Player one throws the ball to bounce at the back of his partner's kicking foot. As the ball bounces behind him, player two flicks the ball back to his partner's hand using his heel.

11 Try numbers 6, 7, 8 and 9, allowing a bounce before striking the ball and hitting the ball just as it leaves the turf. This is called a half-volley.

12 Try numbers 6, 7, 8 and 9, making a dummy jump (kicking out without making contact with the ball) with the non-kicking leg before your first touch of the ball.

13 Player one throws the ball to bounce in front of player two. As the ball bounces player two steps over it, and flicks the ball into the air with the inside of the trailing leg and volleys it back to his partner.

With practice every part of the foot can be used to control and pass the ball

JUGGLING – knocking the ball back and forth in the air without allowing it to touch the ground – and the various tricks that can be used to get the ball into the air without using your hands, may not be something that you use in games. However, learning and practising these techniques are vital ways to develop your confidence and first touch. There is no better practice for developing control using all areas of the body.

Try juggling the ball with your knees, thighs, ankles, heels, head and feet – any part of your body except for your arms and hands.

When you have mastered juggling with an ordinary football you can try using a smaller mini football or *futebol de salão* or a tennis ball to increase difficulty. Pelé used all of these, as well as a grapefruit, to improve the accuracy of his touch.

Juggling exercises can also be done in groups. In Brazil, particularly in Rio, juggling circles are very common. A juggling circle is a small group of men and women, boys and girls who juggle the ball between each other, passing the ball on without letting it touch the ground. Each player tries to use a more extravagant and spectacular trick to keep the ball in the air.

Set yourself weekly targets for improving your juggling skills, not only aiming for a higher number, but looking at achieving higher scores for specific difficult body areas. Remember, this is the best way to improve your first touch.

If you are a beginner you can allow the ball to bounce once or twice on the ground between each touch. As you develop you can take the bounce away.

Here are some juggling exercises you can try:

1 Juggle using only your knees.

2 Juggle the ball with your head.

3 Juggle from shoulder to shoulder.

4 Juggle using only your worst foot.

Lift the shoulders to create a 'cradle' that will hold the ball behind the neck

5 Juggle using only the outside of one foot.

6 While juggling with your feet, try to catch and hold the ball on the foot, on the area above the laces. Cushion the ball as it drops and hold for five seconds. You can also try catching and holding the ball on the area between thigh and stomach.

7 Try catching the ball on the back of your neck or on your forehead. Hold for a few seconds, then return to the juggle.

8 While juggling, allow the ball to bounce on the ground once, step over to the middle, missing the ball, and flick the ball back up with the heel of the trailing leg.

9 While juggling the ball on one foot, bring the foot in a complete circle around the ball as it is in the air, then return to the juggle.

10 While juggling on one foot, take the juggling leg behind the standing leg, flick the ball with it and return to the juggle.

11 Working in pairs, juggle the ball four times and then pass it to your partner. Your partner should receive the ball without allowing it to bounce, juggle four times and pass it back. See how long you can continue this without allowing the ball to touch the ground.

12 While juggling, lean to the side so that the outside edge of your shoe is raised from the ground. Allow the ball to bounce on the outside edge of the shoe and then pick up the juggle.

How to get the ball from the ground to a juggle:

1 With the ball in front of you quickly bring both feet together and under the ball. The spin takes the ball into the air.

2 Take the ball between the inside of both feet (a). Leap up and in mid-air push one foot against the ball, so that it flicks out to the side (b).

3 Again, take the ball between the feet and leap in the air, but this time flick the ball out behind you.

4 Pinch the ball between the back inside of both feet. Leap in the air with the ball, turn and catch the ball on your foot.

5 With the sole of the foot drag the ball back towards your body. Use the same foot as a ramp, allowing the ball to move up the foot and into the air.

6 The kick-start. Stamp the foot hard over one edge of the ball. The ball will lift into the air.

7 With a partner feeding you a rolling ball, step over the ball with one foot (a) and flick the ball into the air with the trailing leg (b).

8 Hit the ball with the heel hard against the standing foot across the body. The ball will lift. A more difficult version of this is to flick the ball behind the standing leg and then to flick it upward with that leg.

The outside of the foot is often used for passing in Brazilian football

BRAZILIAN TEAMS have at their heart good passing. A good pass is made, not just when the ball is hit, but when it's received. The quality of a pass is evident not when it is struck, but by the ease with which your team-mate is able to control it. The perfectly weighted strike sends the ball exactly to where the recipient wants it, where it is brought under control with that exquisite first touch. The secret of good passing is knowing when and where to hit the ball with the correct accuracy and power.

There are many types of pass suitable for different game situations. Experience and practice will help you learn which to use in any given situation. These drills will give you experience in every conceivable type of passing and will serve you well on the pitch.

The aim of these drills is to improve the accuracy of passing. For the first set of drills you will need to work with a partner, standing five metres apart and passing along the ground.

1 Pass the ball between you, using the inside of the foot to kick the ball.

2 Pass the ball using the outside of the foot.

3 Player one passes the ball using the inside or outside of the foot. Player two controls the ball with the sole of one foot and returns with the inside or outside of the other.

4 Player one passes to player two. Player two stops the ball with the sole of the foot, drags it back and takes a second touch with the same foot, playing the ball across, behind the standing leg. He catches the ball with the other foot, drags it across the front of the body on the sole and passes back with the kicking foot.

5 Player one passes to player two. Player two receives the ball and with the side of the foot plays it behind the standing leg, then passes it back with the other foot.

6 Player one drags the ball to the right with the left foot, following through with the body and stopping the ball with the right foot, so that he has moved one step to the side. This move is repeated three times. Player one then passes the ball diagonally to player two and runs back to the starting position. Player two repeats the move, moving three steps to the side then passing diagonally.

Remember, when swerving the ball to the inside or outside you will have to make an allowance for the bend of the ball, which will start to travel in the direction of your foot, but will then swerve away. You should learn to pick a point to aim your kick that will take into account the swerve of the ball. This can only come with practice

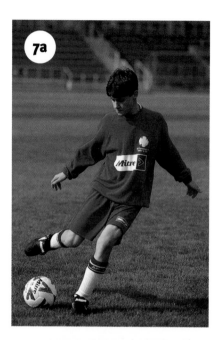

The next set of exercises should be performed with a gap of ten metres between the two players.

7 Kick through the ball with the instep driving it across the floor (a). Your partner touches the ball with the outside of the kicking foot (b) playing it out so it is easy to strike and return with the instep.

8 Repeat exercise 7 but lean back slightly, lifting the ball. Your partner controls the ball with any body part and returns.

The next exercises should be executed ten to twenty-five metres apart, although the age of the players should be taken into account.

9 Drop the ball in front of you and strike it with the laced area of the shoe as it falls. Your partner should catch and return the ball.

10 Repeat exercise 9, using the inside and outside of the foot to create swerve on the volley.

11 Try exercise 9 again and the variations explained in exercise 10, this time striking the ball on the half-volley (i.e. as it comes up from a bounce on the ground).

12 Throw the ball to your side, make an arc with the kicking foot, and kick the ball to your partner on the volley.

In the following exercises, your partner can either catch the ball and return it, or, as you become more experienced, control and return the ball in the manner described.

13 Taking a straight run-up, strike the ball on the top, pushing down through the ball with the instep. This will create backspin. Your partner then takes one touch to chest the ball down, and returns in the same manner.

14 Take an angled run-up and come round the ball, striking it on the far side with the instep. The ball will swing in towards your partner, who should receive the ball on the outside of his foot at knee height, and return it in the same way.

15 Try exercise 14 running up to the ball from the opposite angle, striking the ball with the outside of the foot. The ball is received in the same way.

PASSING DRILLS FOR GROUPS

1 This is basically a form of piggy in the middle. In a small group of five to eight, make a circle. One player goes in the middle and the players around him have to pass the ball between each other without him intercepting it. If the ball is intercepted from your pass, or if you kick the ball out of the circle, then you take over the place in the middle. You can refine the rules, such as each taking two touches or only using your weaker foot. In Brazil this game is played frequently, and if the players manage to put the ball through the legs of the opponent, he is given an extra 'go' in the middle. It is an excellent way to hone your skills, as the passing needs to be of the correct weight and accuracy in order to meet its target.

The next five drills are used by all Brazilian teams. You will require six players for each of the drills and an area roughly a quarter of the size of a full-size pitch. Follow the

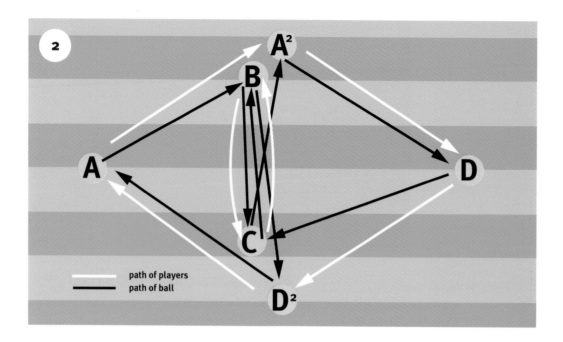

path of players
path of ball

diagrams carefully and walk through the drills initially so that you are clear about where you need to move and pass the ball. In time you will be able to execute these drills with great fluidity and smoothness. You should aim for these drills to be done with one touch, but you may have to work up to this.

Try passing using variations of a one-touch pass, such as a Rivaldo reverse pass. To do this quickly, take the kicking foot behind the standing leg and strike the ball with the instep.

2 The players form two queues, 'A' and 'D' facing each other 20 metres apart. Between them stand two players, 'B' and 'C' facing each other, ten metres apart. 'A' (the player

at the front of queue 'A') plays the ball to 'B', 'B' plays to 'C', 'C' plays to 'A' who has run behind 'B' (to position A2 in the diagram). 'B' and 'C' swap places as they pass. 'A' plays the ball to 'D' (the player at the front of queue 'D') and joins the back of queue 'D'. 'D' plays to 'C', 'C' plays to 'B', 'B' returns the ball to 'D' who has run behind 'C' (position D2). 'B' and 'C' have interchanged positions again as they passed. 'D' plays the ball to the new player at the front of queue 'A' and runs to join that queue. The drill then begins again. Note 'B' and 'C' remain in the middle and only change places with each other. The players in queues 'A' and 'D' are basically running end to end, playing a pass off 'B' or 'C' in the middle of the sequence.

Exercise 2. The player in the foreground starts in position A ...

... having passed the ball to player C from position A2 he moves to D.

From D he moves to position D2 and passes the ball to player B ...

... then returns to position A to complete the move.

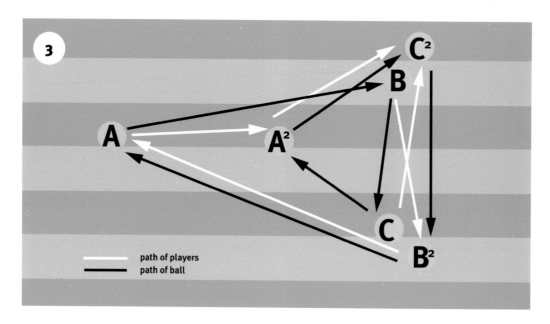

3 key:
- path of players
- path of ball

3 Players 'A', 'B' and 'C' form a triangle with twenty-five metres between 'A' and 'B' and 'C' and ten metres between 'B' and 'C'. The rest of the players form a queue behind 'A'. 'A' plays the ball to 'B' then runs fifteen metres closer to 'B' and 'C' (A2). 'B' passes the ball to 'C' then runs into 'C's position (B2). 'C' passes the ball to 'A' (now in position A2) and runs to 'B's position (C2). 'A' passes the ball back to 'C' (at C2). 'C' passes to 'B' (at B2) who passes the ball back to the new head of the queue and runs to the back of the queue. 'C' runs into the position left by 'B' and 'A' replaces 'C'. For this drill all passes should be played on the floor.

4 The same drill as above but with the two long passes in the drill replaced by lofted drives with back spin.

5 Try drill 2 again, copying the same movements but keeping the ball in the air. The ball is not allowed to touch the ground.

6 Form two queues of three players, facing each other as if in a tug of war. The player at the front of queue one passes to the player at the front of queue two, then runs round to the back of queue two. The player from queue two then repeats this, passing to the new front player of queue one before running to the back of it. The ball should be kept in the air, with each player taking two touches and then passing to the front of the opposite queue before running to the back of that line and awaiting their next turn.

Play the Brazilian Way

Exercise 3. The player at the front of the queue passes to the player in position B (to his left).

He then runs to position A2 while the players in positions B and C exchange the ball.

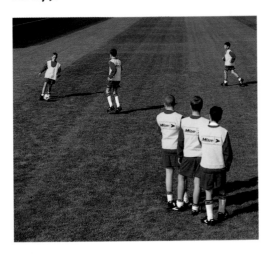

After receiving the ball from player C he passes it back to him, now in position C2, and then takes his place. Player C will pass to B and take his place while B passes back to the front of the queue and joins the queue. The movement then begins again.

THERE IS NOTHING that excites a crowd more than a player who has the ability to dribble and beat players. One of the greatest pleasures in football is to see an attacking player beating defender after defender. Football is a team game, but there is always room for the individual, and dribbling is one art where the individual is able to show the full range of his skills.

THE FOLLOWING EXERCISES WILL HELP
YOU IMPROVE YOUR DRIBBLING:

1 With a partner, take the ball and dribble,
keeping the ball very close to the body, but
moving swiftly. Your partner jockeys you
closely, but does not make an interception.
Work across the pitch. When one partner
has dribbled in one direction, the players
reverse roles and return.

2 Work in threes across the pitch. Player
one carries the ball across the pitch,
touching the ball as many times as he can.
On reaching the other side he passes to
player two who dribbles back across the
pitch and passes to player three. Player
three runs across and passes to player one,
completing the movement.

Balance is the key to dribbling. Crouch low
over the ball so that if you do lose balance,
you can recover quickly. Pelé dribbled
with the ball slightly further back on his
foot than normal. Brazilians in general
tend to use the sole a lot more when
embarking on a mazy run. Pelé's advice is
to dribble with the ball on the foot furthest
from your opponent, keeping your body
between him and the ball. It is very
important to learn to shield the ball
properly. Remember to keep your head up
and never let the ball be more than a
metre from your feet at any time.

It is not speed that counts in dribbling
as much as acceleration, being able to
change pace and burst past an opponent
with an injection of speed. Sudden starts
and stops always fool opponents, but
remember, don't dribble too long, you
can't beat the whole team.

MOVES TO BEAT OPPONENTS

You won't always be able to beat an
opponent in a dribble through speed and
acceleration alone. You need to learn to
trick the opponent, using your feet, body
and ball control to throw them off balance
and keep them guessing.

The ability to go past a player using skill
is something for which Brazilians are
renowned. Players like Zico, Garrincha and
more recently Denílson have the almost
magical ability to manipulate body and ball
in a way which bewitches defenders and
leaves them trailing. This has not come
naturally to the players; these moves are
learned and practised for hours.

In the next section I will describe some of
the tricks Brazilians use to beat their
opponents one on one. I have named each
move after the player who made it famous
or used it most.

All of these moves are used in the game
in a dribbling situation, but they can easily
be practised with a stationary ball, alone or
with a friend acting as an opponent.

Start by practising on your own with a
stationary ball, then on your own with a
moving ball. Later, use a friend as a non-
tackling opponent. The final development is
to work against an opponent who will tackle

The great Carlos Alberto, captain of the 1970 World Cup winning side

and challenge. Soon you will be ready to put these moves into your game.

Even at the earliest stages of learning, never be afraid to try these moves. It is only through trial and error that you will learn. These movements are all about confusing defenders by sending them the wrong way or causing them to lose balance. It is important as you progress to perform the moves with increasing speed. At the highest levels of the game these moves are only successful if executed at lightning speed. An attacking player will have only a split second to accelerate away – the slightest hesitation will allow the defender to regain his composure.

I have described these moves as for a right-footed player but a left-footed player can simply reverse the move. Really talented players will be able to do the moves with either foot.

Carlos Alberto

Alberto was the captain of his club, Santos, and of Brazil in the 1970 triumph in Mexico. During his time with Santos, he and Pelé won almost all of the silverware that a club side can possibly accumulate. Alberto led by example. Furious in the tackle but also adept at attacking from deep positions, his speed and accuracy were deadly. In front of 107,000 people he scored the fourth goal in Brazil's 4–1 World Cup final triumph over Italy in the Azteca stadium in Mexico City, a thundering drive delivered without breaking step after running on to a delightful ball from Pelé. The goal epitomized Brazilian football at its best.

⬤ Dummy as if you are going to pass or cross, then draw the ball back with the inside of your foot behind your standing leg. Wait for your opponent to fall off balance, complete your turn and move away with either your left foot or the outside of your right foot.

Bebeto

After a spell in Spain, Bebeto, one of the heroes of USA 94, is back in Brazil. When Zagallo recalled this mercurial striker for France 98, many criticized his decision, but Bebeto's ability to get around and through the world's best defences makes him a hard man to ignore. However, despite scoring three goals during the competition Bebeto had a poor World Cup - he appeared to lack the pace and agility that four years earlier had made him one of the world's most feared strikers. He is unlikely to play for the national team again but will be remembered for his magnificent contribution to the 1994 World Cup victory.

⬤ Step on the ball with the right foot, then drag it back. Spin round and accelerate off in the opposite direction.

Caréca, one of the best Brazilian players never to have won the World Cup

Caréca

Caréca was a great Brazilian player playing at a time when Brazil didn't have great teams. In 1986 and 1990 he scored plenty of goals leading Brazil's attack, but was let down by the defensive frailties of the team. Tragically, Caréca was injured in training shortly before the 1982 World Cup and had to miss the tournament. He moved from Brazilian club Santos to play at Italian club Napoli, where he partnered Diego Maradona in attack. He now runs his own soccer school in Campinas, São Paulo state.

'Clearly much of European football is all about power and strength. It is not beautiful football. The English need to adopt the Brazilian strategy to a greater extent, and learn to carry the ball to the opposition's goal. I think that the training methods in England need to concentrate more on working with the ball. It should be ball, ball, ball all of the time. Clearly the English do not train enough. In Brazil we train twice every day. Last year an average league team played eighty games, in addition to this the national team played twenty-four games. You cannot play enough football. It makes me smile to hear that the English say that they play too many games. Here in Brazil our rest season is only three weeks!

'I had the opportunity in my career to play with some great players in Santos, São Paulo and Napoli as well as the national team. I had a good relationship with Maradona who partnered me in Napoli; our understanding was good on and off the pitch. Playing in Italy made me more of a complete player. The European style and slower Brazilian style were different. My performances in the national team reflected both styles and I improved as a player because of my experience in Europe.'

Caréca

● Step on the ball with the right foot. Jump over, turning around to your left with your back to the ball.

Denílson

Denílson, like Juninho, developed his skills playing futebol de salão *in São Paulo. He joined São Paulo FC as a junior player and was playing in the first team before his eighteenth birthday. He was called up to the Brazilian national team for the 1997 Tournoi de France and had an outstanding tournament, prompting many of Europe's top clubs to scramble for his signature. He finally signed for Spanish side Real Betis for a record-breaking £23 million. This left-sided attacker has outstanding dribbling skills, and is rightly compared in Brazil to that earlier legend, Garrincha.*

● Step on the ball with your right foot turning to your left, catch the ball on the heel of your left foot and accelerate away.

'I believe São Paulo has the best training in the world and has prepared me well. I came out of futebol de salão *and developed my skills in this way of football and play in the same way now as I did on the* futebol de salão *courts'*

Denílson

'The true and total beauty of football is only seen in the ingenuity, inventiveness, instinct and skill of the players, both individually and as a team. This can only be seen in an attacking style of football, when the ball is always under control. A long kick the length of the field, hoping a team-mate will first reach the ball or head it into the net can hardly be called artistic'

Pelé

Didi

The Great Didi (Waldyr Pereira) was known for his elegance and mastery of the ball. He first played for Brazil in 1952 and became a world champion with the team in 1958 and 1962. Didi was considered as Brazil's finest-ever player until Pelé came along. His genius was his creativity but unlike many gifted playmakers he also had athleticism and a great fitness that allowed him to show his skills all over the pitch right through the game. Even in his later years as a player, when his pace had slowed, he was still able to command a huge influence on a game. He was a great success at Rio club sides Botafogo and Fluminense. He managed the Peruvian national side knocked out by Brazil in the 1970 World Cup.

⬤ Bring the foot back and lift the arms as though about to shoot. As the foot is about to strike the ball quickly turn the foot and bring the ball away in the opposite direction with the outside of the foot.

Dodô

This player is currently with São Paulo FC. He has not yet played for Brazil, but he has many admirers, and Zagallo came in for much criticism for not selecting him for the squad for France 98.

⬤ Take the right foot half over the ball as though moving away. Quickly pull out and knock the ball back in the opposite direction with the outside of the right foot.

Emerson

Emerson Moises da Costa is a hugely talented midfielder, who played in Portugal with Belenenses and Porto before joining Middlesbrough in the summer of 1996, where he played in the same team as Juninho and Ravanelli before leaving for Tenerife in January 1998. He has a ferocious shot and a repertoire of tricks which he is never afraid to execute, even during the most competitive games.

The move which mesmerised English defences

The final stage of Emerson 3

1 Hit the ball hard with the inside of one foot so that it rebounds hard off the inside of the other foot and takes you in the other direction with the ball, away from the confused defender.

2 Take the left leg to the middle of the body over the ball and at the same time scoop the ball away, hitting it with the inside of the right foot behind the left leg.

3 Kick the ball behind the standing leg with the side of the foot. Flick the ball back in front of the body with the outside of the same foot.

Falcão

Few who witnessed the 1982 World Cup finals will forget the midfield sensation that was Falcão. An inventive player, Falcão combined well with Zico in Brazil's attack. He later became manager of the Brazilian national team for a short time, but did not enjoy the same success as a manager as he had enjoyed as a player.

● Running with the ball, stop the ball with the sole of the foot, rolling it back and then positioning the foot so that the laces area taps the ball forward. This must be performed in one move.

Garrincha

A childhood illness left Garrincha's legs badly twisted. Doctors thought that he would do well merely to be able to walk. Garrincha, nicknamed 'The Little Bird', did much more than walk, he became one of the quickest and most dangerous wingers of all time. In many respects, the story of Garrincha is one of tragedy and triumph. Manoel Francisco dos Santos, to give him his full name, joined Pau Grande at the age of fourteen. He later played for Botafogo, Corinthians, Flamengo and Red Star Paris. However, it was his international success in winning the World Cup with Brazil in 1958 and 1962 that made Garrincha a world star. His mazy dribbles down the left side amazed the watching world. Garrincha died in truly tragic circumstances – his hospital death certificate stated 'Name Unknown' – but he will never be forgotten in Brazil or by anyone who saw this magical footballer.

● Drop the right shoulder and bend the right knee behind the ball (a). Transfer the body weight quickly to the left side of the body and come away with the outside of the left foot, leaving the defender off balance (b).

An easy move to learn, but very effective at throwing defenders off balance

Gerson

Gerson sat at the heart of Brazil's midfield during the Mexico 1970 World Cup finals. His passing from midfield was sublime, but he also possessed a powerful shot. He began his career with Flamengo, later moving to Botafogo and finally São Paulo. He made eighty-four appearances for Brazil and played in both the 1966 and 1970 World Cups.

1 Running with the ball, stop the ball with the sole of the left foot before kicking it on immediately with the toe of the right foot. This stop-start motion will cause the defender to stop dead, leaving you with room to shoot or pass. This move was used effectively by Romário against Manchester United in the Champions' League in 1995.

2 Running with the ball, fake a backheel, missing the ball (a), then touching it on with the toe of the same foot (b).

Here the player steps over the ball with the left leg, then the right leg, then again with the left

Jairzinho, the only player ever to have scored in every round of the World Cup

Jairzinho

Jairzinho first signed professional forms for Botafogo when he was only fifteen. He had a tough childhood and football was an escape for him. His performance in the 1970 World Cup marked his name indelibly in the record books, as he became the first player to score in every round of the tournament. He later played for Marseille, but was not suited to European football, and returned to Brazil with Portuguesa. In eighty-seven full internationals he scored thirty-eight goals. He is still known as Jairzinho, a name famous throughout the world, rather than his full name of Jair Ventura Filho.

Step over the ball to the outside with the right foot, then step over with the left foot to the outside before taking the ball away with the outside of the right foot. These step-overs can be performed as many times as you wish, as was demonstrated by Denílson in the 1998 World Cup final.

Juninho

Juninho began playing football at the age of two in his own home, prompted by his father, who had been a trialist with São Paulo club Palmeiras until an injury ended his hopes of a footballing career. Until the age of fourteen, Juninho played only futebol de salão. He joined São Paulo club Ituano at that age, and went on to join São Paulo FC at the age of twenty. He played his first game for Brazil in 1995 against Slovakia and that year was voted Brazilian Footballer of the Year. His performances, particularly against England in the Umbro Cup in the summer of

Juninho racing away with the ball during the 1995 Umbro Cup in England

1995, alerted Middlesbrough manager Bryan Robson to his abilities, and in November 1995 he signed for Middlesbrough. His time at the club came to an end at the end of the 1996/7 season with the relegation of his team. He then moved to Spanish giants Atletico Madrid, primarily because he felt his international career would be in jeopardy in a World Cup year if he were not playing top-flight football. However, an injury led to his absence from the Madrid side for the crucial three months prior to coach Mario Zagallo announcing his team. Zagallo said that he couldn't take the risk, and Juninho missed out on his greatest ambition, to represent his country in the world's biggest sporting showcase.

1 Shield the ball, holding the left arm against the defender. Turn the ball 180 degrees with the inside of the right foot. Do not let the ball leave your foot at any point. Either take the ball between you and the defender or play it through the defender's legs and accelerate away.

2 When receiving the ball step over it with your left foot and accelerate away with the ball on your right foot.

3 As with the Denílson move, step on the ball with your right foot (a) jumping to your left, but catch the ball with the sole rather than the heel of the left foot (b) and accelerate away.

Junior

Junior played almost his entire career with Flamengo. Former national team coach Claudio Coutinho converted Junior from a midfielder into one of football's first attacking full backs (wing backs). In the new position, Junior was devastatingly effective; a strong defender but also an explosive attacking force. He won over fifty caps for Brazil and played in the 1982 and 1986 World Cups.

● Step over the ball to the outside with the right foot. Shift the weight back to the left side of the body and come away with the ball on the outside of the left foot.

Leonardo

Another master Brazilian midfielder, his influence and his ability to control a game from the middle of the field has carved out a career for him in Brazil, Italy and Japan. Another of Zagallo's controversial choices for France 98, but few national squads would refuse the services of such an elegant, skilful and accomplished player.

● This is similar to the second Emerson move, but the ball is knocked away through the legs of your opponent. This requires practice and can only be attempted after the second Emerson move has been perfected.

Marcelinho

Marcelinho (Marcel Carioca) is the current rising star of Brazilian football. Playing at number seven for Brazil and club side Corinthians, Marcelinho is renowned for his intelligent passing, speed and dribbling ability. He is regarded as the best player in the Brazilian league and will surely move in the near future to the Spanish or Italian league.

● Step behind the ball with the left foot, over the ball with the right foot, and come away, taking the ball with the outside of the left foot.

Pelé

The boy who would become known throughout the world as 'Pelé' was christened Edson Arantes do Nascimento. Legend suggests that he learned the game on the backstreets of his hometown, Tres Coraçōes, with balls made of old rags stuffed with socks, but this is not the whole story. His father Dondinho, who had been a promising footballer before injury ended his career, tutored Pelé in the art of football. Pelé's schooldays were spent playing futebol de salāo. Aged ten, he joined his first club, Baurú, where his father was coach. Five years later, he made his league debut for São Paulo team Santos. A year after that, he lined up in his first international match for Brazil against their arch-rivals Argentina. In 1958 he was part of

Pelé, the world's greatest ever footballer, with the Jules Rimet Trophy

the World Cup-winning Brazilian team.

Three World Cup victories (1958, 1962 and 1970), wonderful skill and a record number of goals in Brazil have earned Pelé the reputation of being the greatest-ever footballer. A poor boy whose talents lifted him to the peaks of achievement, fame and riches, Pelé retained his sense of sportsmanship, his desire to entertain his fans, his love of the game and the respect of his fellow players. Now Minister of Sport in Brazil, he remains a great example and inspiration to children around the world.

'When I see beautiful football, I am happy. Sadly, today most coaches' first thinking is to try not to lose, rather than to win. I find fault with defensive football because the best way to score goals is to have possession of the ball. Ball control to me is the most important tactic in the game.

'Defensive football trades ball control for apparent safety in the goal areas. The long goal kick or clearance, supposed to be away from danger, often falls to the opposition as the defensive team has few forwards far down the field. This move I admit is occasionally necessary, but should never be employed as a standard tactic. Possession and control of the ball are the key tactics for children and adults alike. This is why futebol de salão is so important.

'The true and total beauty of football is only seen in the ingenuity, inventiveness, instinct and skill of the players, both individually and as a team. This can only be seen in an attacking style of football, when the ball is always under control. A long kick the length of the field, hoping a team-mate will first reach the ball or head it into the net can hardly be called artistic. Besides, for the fans nothing compares to the spectacle of attacking football.

'Young people need to train with the ball constantly. You also need to have the right people around you. If children are shown proper exercises and training methods, techniques of dribbling, passing, control, moves to beat players and shooting, they will understand that all players can develop skills regardless of their nationality.

'I played futebol de salão growing up in Baurú. In my area the game was first played outdoors on a hard basketball court and was sponsored by the local radio station. Later we played the game indoors. It made for an extremely fast game. I played this game for my juvenile teams Radium and Noroestinho at fourteen. The following year I signed for Santos. In futebol de salão you need to think quick and play quick so it's easier for you when you move to normal football.'

Pelé

1 Drag the ball with the sole of the right foot from right to left and cannon it off the inside of the left foot while the right leg continues its forward movement.

2 Stop the ball between both feet (a), grip it tightly and jump past the opponent (b).

3 Again stop the ball and grip it tightly between the feet (a), then lift both feet behind you, turning them towards your opponent when airborne (b) and release the ball. The ball will be thrown over the head of your opponent so you can run on to it.

Petá

Many São Paulo supporters regard Petá as one of the finest players in their club's recent history. During the 1980s he terrorized defences in the São Paulo and Brazilian leagues with his incisive passing and devastating dribbles. He played only a few games for the Brazilian national team but is regarded as a living legend at São Paulo where he currently works as a coach with the club's junior team.

⬤ With the side of the right foot, push the ball as far out as your left leg will extend. Do not let your foot lose touch with the ball. You will find that your sole is now on top of the ball. Drag the ball back with your right foot and push away.

Rivelino

Rivelino spent many long hours as a child practising free kicks and shooting skills, the same skills that would later become legendary throughout the world as his spectacular set plays became one of the hallmarks of the Brazilian teams of the 1970s. He played for club sides Corinthians and Fluminense, but it was his international performances which made him a legend. The 1970 World Cup is remembered not only for the flair of Pelé and the goals of Jairzinho but also for the explosive shooting of

Rivelino. He represented Brazil ninety-four times, scoring twenty-six goals and playing in three World Cups (1970, 1974 and 1978). Rivelino was a deeply religious and superstitious man and claimed that as long as he kept his large and rather extravagant moustache, Brazil would not lose.

'I think that talent comes from God, and even with the best coaching it is difficult to turn a player without ability into a world star. But if the player has some ability, the coach can bring that out, and even bad

players can become good players through good coaching.

'It is important that the young player works always with the ball. Small-sided games are the best environment in which you can develop skills. As well as training, attitude and philosophy are also important.

'The game is faster today than it was in the 1970s and there is a greater importance given to fitness and strength, but you need to impose your style of play on the opposition, and not vice versa.'

Rivelino

1 Step over the ball to the inside with your right foot. Bring the ball away with the outside of the same foot.

2 The Rivelino Elastic: strike the ball to the outside with the toes, keep a grip on the ball and bring it back across the body to the inside. Beginners can use the sole of the foot to help perform the first part of this move. It must be performed in one movement.

Romário in the 1994 World Cup final

Play the Brazilian Way

Romário

The powerful Romário comes from a poor family in Rio de Janeiro. He first played for Brazil in 1987, while playing for Brazilian club Vasco da Gama. He later moved to Dutch side PSV Eindhoven, then Barcelona, Valencia before arriving at Flamengo, the club he had supported as a boy in Rio de Janeiro. He inspired Brazil to their fourth World Cup win in the USA in 1994. His ability to move at lightning speed with superb close control made Romário the World Player of the Year in 1994. After the finals, Romário suffered from a run of poor form, but was later recalled to the national team by coach Mario Zagallo in a bid for further World Cup glory in France 1998. His hopes of World Cup glory were dashed when Zagallo dropped him from the squad, ostensibly as a result of an injury incurred playing beach football. As always with Romário, there was controversy surrounding this decision, and he was playing club football in Brazil once again before the World Cup started.

● Running with the ball, backheel the ball with your right foot on to the front of your left ankle. The ball runs on and the defender is left rooted to the spot.

Ronaldo

Ronaldo learned his skills playing futebol de salão *for Social Ramos. He later moved to São Cristóvão after being rejected by Rio de Janeiro's biggest club, Flamengo. It was at Cruzeiro that he first gained national attention, scoring fifty-four goals in fifty-four games. This was the catalyst that prompted PSV Eindhoven to sign Ronaldo for £4 million, a record for a seventeen-year-old. In the same year, he was part of the Brazilian squad for the 1994 World Cup in the USA, but he did not feature in any of the games. Since then, he has been Brazil's first-choice striker, and has moved clubs on two occasions, first to Barcelona, then to Inter Milan for £18 million. He was voted World Footballer of the Year in 1997 and 1998.*

Ronaldo played through the 1998 World Cup with a knee injury. This, and the pressure of expectations and sponsorship commitments appeared to affect Ronaldo and he fell ill on the day of the final against France. He was at first pulled out of the team, but later reinstated. Brazil played poorly and it was clear that Ronaldo's team-mates were concerned about his illness. Ronaldo scored four goals in the competition and showed some flashes of the ability that made him World Player of the Year. As a young man he has plenty of time to return from the setback of the 1998 World Cup final and re-establish himself as the best player in the world.

Ronaldo, the most feared attacking force in world football

Socrates

Socrates' football fame was gained with São Paulo team Corinthians. He captained Brazil in the 1982 and 1986 World Cups. Playing either in midfield or attack, he demonstrated superb creative powers and intelligence.

1 Drag the ball back with the sole of your right foot and knock it with the side of your right foot behind your standing left leg.

2 Repeat the above, but complete the manoeuvre in one movement.

Tostão

Eduardo Gonçalves was a player with Cruzeiro and Vasco da Gama. He made his full international debut in England for Brazil during the 1966 World Cup. An horrific eye injury in 1969 put his participation in the 1970 World Cup in doubt. However, after a specialist operation in the United States, he returned in glory as a vital part of the triumphant 1970 side. To avoid further injury to his eye, he retired in 1973 at the age of twenty-six. He did, however, have another career to fall back on. He is a doctor. Perhaps fittingly, he later became a prominent eye specialist.

● Drag the ball across the body with the sole of the right foot (a). Meet the ball with the left foot (b). You can either take the ball away with the left foot or take the left foot over the ball and take the ball away with the right foot.

● Standing or running with the ball to the outside of your right foot, turn to your left and hook the ball away with the front of your left foot.

Vavá

Vavá was the Brazilian centre forward during the successful 1958 and 1962 World Cup campaigns. He scored nine goals in those tournaments, and was the first player to score in the final of two successive World Cups. Vasco da Gama was his first Brazilian club side and he later played for Atletico Madrid, before returning to Brazil with Palmeiras.

⬤ Twist the knee and shape the hips to the right, as though playing the ball, but come away in the opposite direction, playing the ball with the inside of the left foot. An extension of this is to step over the ball to the middle with the right foot before coming away with the side of the left foot.

Zico, one of history's greatest midfielders

Zico

Artur Antunes Coimbra was known as the 'White Pelé' because of his similar style and breathtaking ability. He had tremendous pace and was renowned for his passing and the accuracy of his free kicks. His goals were nothing less than sensational. Zico even managed to score on his international debut in 1975.

This wiry attacker is regarded as the best Brazilian footballer never to win a World Cup winners' medal. He scored fifty-four goals for Brazil, a record bettered only by Pelé. One of his proudest moments came in 1983, when he was named 'World Footballer of the Year'. He had other great successes,

particularly with Flamengo, who won the World Club Championship in 1981 in Tokyo. He also played for Italian side Udinese and Kashima Antlers in Japan. The world remembers Zico for his participation in Brazil's quest for World Cup glory in 1982 but he also took part in the 1978 and 1986 finals. After retiring from football, he enjoyed a short spell as Brazil's minister of sport, before founding his own soccer school for children in Rio de Janeiro. He was Brazil's assistant coach for France 98.

'As a kid, the only game I played was futebol de salão. It is the best environment for producing excellent players, as you need to think and play quickly, because the ball is always on the floor. When I was young it was difficult to find a grass pitch. Now those areas are impossible to find. The most important thing for children is that they enjoy playing football. My method is typical of all training in Brazil. It is ball, ball, and only ball. With kids of five, six and seven years they need to be working every day with the ball. When you get to fourteen or fifteen it's OK to start looking at tactics, but first you should only concentrate on the ball.

'I myself came out of futebol de salão. This is all that my brothers and I played as kids. In futebol de salão you need to think quick, play quick and, because the ball is always on the floor, it is the best environment for producing excellent players. All of the Brazilian players graduated from this type of football.

'As for the future, it's difficult to predict what will happen. I think that the Japanese may become very strong. They are improving very quickly and putting the right emphasis on training and preparation. I am also very impressed with the African nations. They remind me a lot of Brazil and indeed some of them are employing Brazilian coaches. It would not surprise me to see Africa emerge as a major force in football. I do not see that much English league football, but from what I know they still play with the ball too much in the air, they need to work on technique and passing of the ball to a greater extent. As other countries improve so Brazil must strive to stay ahead of the pack. I am sure that we will.'

Zico

1 Shape the body as though about to strike the ball for a shot or cross. Miss the ball and with the outside of the kicking foot, knock it through the legs of the opponent.

2 This move is essentially the same as the Rivelino Elastic, except you first move the ball to the inside of your body before pushing it to the outside and away from the defender.

Always keep your eye on the ball when shooting

MIDFIELD WIZARDRY, passing and dribbling skills have given Brazilian football its position as the epitome of Pelé's 'beautiful game', but whether defender, attacker or midfielder, the ability to shoot is an essential part of the good footballer's make-up. Who can forget the marvellous shooting of Rivelino, the accuracy of Pelé or the wicked swerve placed on a ball by Roberto Carlos?

These skills are gained through hours and hours of practice. The most important part of shooting is to ensure that you hit the target and commit the goalkeeper to make a save. Any shot needs power and accuracy if it is to beat a goalkeeper, but sometimes accuracy is more important than force, particularly from close range.

Push pass/shot – outside: a trademark of the Brazilian game

Push pass/shot – inside

Strike the ball with the whole inside of the foot, crouch slightly, with your arms outstretched for good balance. The non-kicking foot should be alongside the ball with the knee slightly bent.

Push pass/shot – outside

This is a very common pass in Brazil, though it is hardly used in Europe. The non-kicking foot should be alongside the ball with the knee slightly bent. Strike the ball with the whole outside of the foot. Crouch slightly, arms outstretched for good balance.

KICKING TECHNIQUES

If you want a shot or pass to go high or low you will need to alter your body position. Leaning back will result in a higher ball, while bending low over the ball keeps the ball low. There are many different ways of striking the ball and the following is a list of the main techniques to master. Always practise using both feet. Brazilian coaches tend to encourage players only to be one-footed – they work on mastering the skills with their strongest foot only. But it is also important to concentrate on your weaker foot.

The non-kicking foot is most important as it can affect accuracy and power. It should be positioned next to the ball as the ball is struck, not behind or in front of it. Make sure it points in the direction you want the ball to travel. To ensure you hit the ball cleanly, keep your eyes on the ball at all times. Remember to follow through with your kicking foot after you have struck the ball.

Low drive/instep drive

Put the non-kicking foot alongside the ball. Draw the kicking foot back as far as possible. Strike the ball with the instep well over the ball, keeping the arms outstretched for balance.

Half-volley

Strike the ball with the instep just as it touches the ground. Keep the head down if you want the ball to remain low. Lean slightly back to produce a higher ball. Judgement of the ball's flight, pace and bounce is essential. This shot can cause goalkeepers problems, especially on difficult surfaces. It is not as powerful as the upright volley.

Volley

Strike the ball with the instep before it touches the ground, at a height of about 30–40cm. The ball should be met strongly, with the weight of the body over it as much as is possible. Keep your eyes on the ball.

Side volley

The side volley is played with the body side-on and the kicking leg extended horizontally. Turn your body into the ball, pivoting on the non-kicking leg. Keep your head facing down to keep the ball low.

Flying sideways volley

Take off from the kicking foot, turn in mid-air and strike the ball with the instep while horizontal. The non-kicking foot is also almost

Side volley (top) and flying side volley (bottom)

horizontal but behind the kicking foot at the moment of impact. Take care on landing.

Chip or lofted kick

Lean the body slightly backward. Kick with the instep, but with toe pointing across the ball rather than downward. Aim to hit the lower half of the ball. Keep the arms outstretched for balance.

Curvita

Turn your kicking foot outward until the inside of your foot faces forward. Raise your foot slightly off the ground and with a smooth firm swing contact the centre of the ball with the inside front of the foot.

Trivella

Use the outside three toes on the edge of your foot. Kick the ball forward or to the side with a pronounced knee action. Lean your body forward into the pass and strike the ball before you lift your weight to your front foot.

Remember: the position of your non-kicking foot will determine the power and accuracy of the kick.

Check where you are targeting the ball before striking it, but keep your eye on the ball when you are making the kick.

Gol de lectra

Standing with your back to the goal when receiving the ball, knock the ball with the side of your right foot at an angle behind your standing left leg into the goal.

The trivella: used to bend the ball around a defensive wall

The non-kicking leg must be airborne when executing the bicycle kick

Bicycle kick

Take off from the kicking foot, swing the non-kicking foot over for leverage, throw the head back and arch your back as you attempt to strike the ball with the instep. Take care on landing.

The following two shots, made famous by Zico, are both executed from a ball crossed from the wings into the penalty area. The player executing the shot is facing the ball, side-on to the goal.

1 Strike the ball on the volley with the inside of the right foot, sending the ball behind the left leg and goal-bound.

2 Flick the ball with the outside of the right foot into the goal, turning 180 degrees towards the goal as you strike the ball.

Dip

Strike the ball with the instep at the bottom of the ball, lifting the foot quickly on contact, up through the ball. With practice you may produce the dip effect that countless Brazilian teams have used to beat defensive walls in free-kick situations. The shot is just as effective when trying to beat an advancing keeper who has come off his line.

A shot with which dips can be a devastatingly effective way to beat a defensive wall from a free kick

HEADING IS A SKILL requiring the coordination of the entire body. It is used to pass, shoot on goal, and, defensively, to clear the ball or intercept an opponent's pass. You can head the ball when standing, running, jumping and even diving. A skilled header of the ball can move the ball forwards, backwards, sideways and at different heights. Using your head to strike a ball is not a natural action, the natural reflex of the head is to move away from a moving object, so it needs extra practice to make it a natural and instinctive movement.

It is easy to overcome the natural fear of heading the ball by throwing the ball on to the centre of your forehead. Once children realize that this does not hurt, the skill can be learned quickly. Although the natural reaction is to blink as the ball comes near, it is important to keep your eyes open until the ball strikes the centre of the forehead. The top of the head should never be used to strike the ball. Always keep your mouth closed to avoid injury.

Standing header

● This can be used to pass the ball or to shoot. Push your body up from your knees when contacting the ball with the centre of your forehead.

Power header

● This shooting header allows you to hit the ball with significant force. Stand with one foot slightly in front of the other and lean back from your waist. Thrust the top half of your body in a forward motion so that the power does not solely come from your neck muscles. Your entire body should follow through after the ball is hit. Practise these movements without the ball first.

Jumping header

● This requires body, arm, head and leg movements at the same time. It is often the more skilled player, not the taller one, who will get the ball first. A beginner should practise with both feet before graduating to the one-footed jump. Initially, practise the

movements for the jumping header without the ball. Run a short distance and leap skywards. Swing back your arms and then thrust them forward and upward as your body lifts from the ground. Lean the top half of the body back from the waist, bend your knees and lift your legs behind your body. Thrust your arms down as your head comes towards the ball. This arm-thrusting will give you the feeling of stopping while airborne. Quickly snap the upper part of your body forward from your waist. Use the neck muscles to drive your head into the ball. When landing, sprint forward to keep balance and avoid injury. Remember – direction will come from the neck. Turn the neck to send the ball to the left or right.

Diving header

● This is used in congested penalty boxes either to score, or, more rarely, to clear the ball. Fling your body full length so that the centre of your forehead connects with the ball. Use the neck muscles to thrust the head forward at the moment of contact. Your body should be horizontal to the ground with the hands moving forward to cushion the fall. Only players who have mastered the standing, jumping and power headers should attempt this action.

Futevolei: *a great game for improving first touch*

THE BRAZILIAN METHOD of training that we have looked at in this book works best if the exercises and drills are broken up with regular playing practice in a small-sided game situation, so that the players can put the skills they are developing into practice. Here are a few different ways that you can do this.

GAMES WITH SMALL GOALS

Play a game of six- or seven-a-side, but use cones to make the goals only one metre wide. This encourages incisive passing and imagination in breaking down the defence.

Games with small goals can be played with the additional rule that each player must have one touch before the team is allowed to take a shot on goal.

POSSESSION FOOTBALL

Play anything between two- and eight-a-side without goals. This is a great way to learn the art of manoeuvring the opposition out of position by keeping possession of the ball.

FUTEVOLEI

For this game you need a badminton net. You can play on grass, tarmac or even on the beach. It is a great way to improve your first touch in a fun environment. Using any part of the body other than the arms or hands, share the ball as a team and then send it over the net. You score a point when the opposition loses control of the ball, but there are no hard and fast rules, you can invent your own. Try the game allowing one bounce between each touch at first and build up to playing the game without bounces between touches. Play games from two-to six-a-side.

FUTEBOL DE SALÃO

'This [futebol de salão] *is how I really got started. This is my love, the thing that I enjoyed most.'* Ronaldo

Futebol de salão is a five-a-side game unique to Brazil. It is taught in every school in Brazil and all the great Brazilian players were brought up playing the game. Most agree that it is *futebol de salão* that is responsible for the spectacular style and skills that Brazilians are so famous for.

It is an ingeniously condensed version of the outdoor game of football that preserves the outdoor game's true time and space relationships. The ball handling, speed, skill and quick thinking of *futebol de salão* translate directly to the outdoor game. The game is the best skill-building environment for football. It develops the specific skills of dribbling, passing, touch and close control – the skills for which Brazilian football is best known.

The ball

The most important ingredient in *futebol de salão* is the ball. It is smaller than a conventional football (a size two, while a conventional ball is a size five). Due to the ball's small size, a greater degree of control and precision is needed to dribble and pass it, but when you have mastered the skills and you switch to the outdoor game you will find dribbling and movements with a conventional football easy.

A game of futebol de salão at the Ayrton Senna Soccer School

The bladder of the *futebol de salão* ball is filled with foam, which makes it heavier than a conventional ball. This means it does not bounce above the ankle. This places a greater emphasis on playing the ball along the ground, rather than making long, high passes. Paradoxically the weighted ball is easier to control from a pass, and this helps to develop a good first touch.

One experienced director of one of the new FA Soccer Academies said of *futebol de salão*:

'I can see why this works. Playing with a normal ball you can get away with the ball bobbling about a bit, but you don't get a lucky bounce with a ball that doesn't bounce. You have to drill the passes, drive the ball, and this makes the passing hard and accurate.

The player receiving the ball has to bring it under control immediately – you don't get a second chance. You have to be accurate, and it shows the way the youngsters play the ball about.'

The court

Futebol de salão is played on a basketball- or netball-sized court (25–30 x 15–17 metres). The small size of the court means that the players are very close to each other, so the whole court is as congested as the penalty area can be in the outdoor game. This means you need to think quickly and play quickly. The game encourages quick decision-making so when you come to play normal football it's easy to cope with the pressure.

The size of the court also encourages creativity and accuracy. You learn to find new

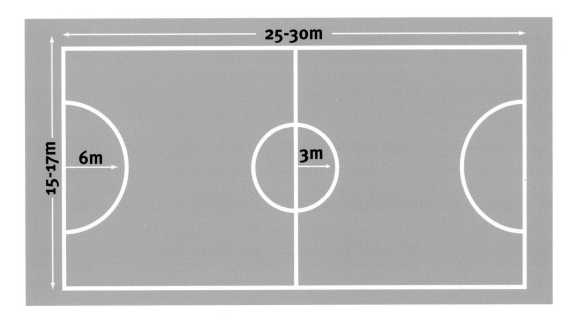

angles and control and pass the ball quickly and precisely. The small playing area and close proximity of opponents teaches players to move and create free space when not on the ball.

The game requires a true, smooth, flat, hard surface such as wood, synthetic material or concrete and should not be played on grass. Playing on a rough surface would result in a slower, imprecise game.

The game can be played indoors or outdoors since unlike in the British five-a-side game, the ball cannot be played off the walls. Playing off the walls encourages players to develop sloppy habits. When playing with walls you don't have to be thorough or accurate when clearing a ball, a thump against the wall will suffice. Passes can be overhit and may still hit the wall and reach your player. A player playing *futebol de salão* will have, on average, two hundred times as many touches of the ball during a game than a player playing an English-style five-a-side with a conventional ball will.

Futebol de salão requires pinpoint-accurate passing through the smallest of spaces. The necessity of keeping the ball in play obligates the players to be more precise in their touches and passes.

The goal

The goal is three metres wide and two metres high. The small goal helps to develop precise shooting.

The team

Each team consists of five players. One player is the goalkeeper, the rest constantly rotate positions, taking defensive and attacking roles as required. This means that players have equal opportunity to develop attacking and defending skills, rather than getting stuck in one position too soon. The use of five players on the smaller playing area ensures that all the players participate fully and accelerates the acquisition of technique.

Each team can have up to seven reserves on the bench. There is no limit to the number of substitutions that can be made during a game. Substitutions can be made while the ball is in play, except when substituting the goalkeeper, as long as the player to be substituted has left the pitch before the substitute joins it.

Kit is the normal football apparel with trainers rather than football boots.

The rules

Futebol de salão is played very much like ordinary football, with the following exceptions:

If the ball goes out of play along the sides of the pitch the game is restarted with a kick-in.

If the ball crosses the goal line after being played by an attacking player then the restart is from a throw by the goalkeeper (this must not cross the half-way line). A goal can not be scored directly from a goal clearance, kick-in or indirect free kick.

As in football, corner kicks are awarded when a defending player puts the ball out of play behind his own goal line. The defenders must be at least three metres from the ball when a free kick, goal kick or corner is taken.

Sliding tackles are not permitted.

The ball must not be headed.

Players who commit more than five culminative fouls during the game will be expelled. After two minutes, or when they have conceded a goal, the team can replace the expelled player with a substitute.

If one team commits more than five fouls during one half, the punishment for a foul will change from an indirect free kick to a direct free kick. After the sixth foul the team is prohibited from forming a defensive wall at a free kick.

A game consists of two halves of twenty minutes for adults or, for young children, two halves of fifteen minutes. As well as a ten-minute break at half-time, each team can take one one-minute break in each half to allow the coach to give instructions to the players. The coach signals for a break with the time out signal (making a T shape with the hands, as in baseball). The break will then be taken next time the ball goes out of play.

In training you can introduce any number of variations to these rules. For instance, try allowing players only one or two touches, or using only their poorer foot.

You can use the *futebol de salão* court and ball to play the possession or small-goal games mentioned above. The *futebol de salão* court can also be used for games of possession football. Divide the court into areas of ten metres by ten metres. In each area play two versus one or three against two. The aim is to keep the ball. It's difficult in such tight spaces but practising in these small areas will make playing on a wide open pitch easier. The key point is to ensure that you are putting the skills you have learned into practice in game situations.

Futebol de salão is well designed for school and recreational play. It costs virtually nothing to stage, since it uses existing facilities. It is a very safe game that emphasizes skill rather than physical contact. As fast-moving and exciting as basketball, it is an excellent spectator sport. Most important of all, it is great fun to play!

If you want to know more about *futebol de salão* you can contact the UK Confederation of Futebol de Salão . The confederation organizes school and club regional and national leagues as well as coaching courses for teachers and coaches. Their aim is to ensure that all British children will be able to benefit from *futebol de salão*.

The UK Confederation of Futebol de Salão produces a quarterly magazine, *Futebol,* as well as a rule book and other coaching material.

Brazilian Soccer Schools are now based in most cities in the UK. They teach children to play football the Brazilian way, through Brazilian coaching methods, *futebol de salão* and *futevolei*. The ambition of the clubs is to create a new and exciting type of British footballer for the future.

For more infomation contact:
The UK Confederation of Futebol de Salão
34 Chandos Place
Leeds
West Yorkshire LS8 1QS
www.futebol-de-salao.co.uk

Conclusion

Brazilian footballers play with grace, beauty, skill, determination and passion, not because they are a poor nation or because they are naturally skilful. Brazilians play like no others because they train and practise like no others. Their training revolves around developing skills, fluidity of movement and mastery of the ball.

All of these elements can be learned and developed through the training techniques described in this book, and by playing *futebol de salão*. With determination and hard work all footballers can learn to play just as beautifully as Brazilians.

It is my dream that in ten or twenty years' time we will have British national teams that will play with as much flair and beauty as Brazilians. If we can ally British determination and tenacity to Brazilian flair we will again be a match for anybody in the arena of international football. The *futebol de salão* revolution and the adoption of Brazilian training methods will make my dream a reality. The legacy of Charles Miller will have come full circle. Football will truly come home.